MONSIEUR
SEEKS A WIFE

BY
MARGARET IRWIN

British Library Cataloguing-in-Publication Data
A catalogue record for this book is available from the
British Library

CONTENTS

MARGARET IRWIN

Margaret Emma Faith Irwin was born in London, England in 1889. She attended Clifton High School in Bristol, followed by Oxford University. She began writing books and short stories in the early 1920s, and married children's author and illustrator John Robert Monsell in 1929. Irwin's 'Queen Elizabeth Trilogy' – comprised of Young Bess (1944), Elizabeth, Captive Princess (1948) and Elizabeth and the Prince of Spain (1953) – were esteemed for the accuracy of their historical research (amongst other things, she meticulously researched Elizabethan slang and conversational stylings), and Irwin became a noted authority on the Elizabethan and early Stewart era. Her The Proud Servant (1949) was also very popular, and saw readers captivated by the charismatic Earl of Montrose. Of her short fiction, 'The Book' (1930), 'Monsieur Seeks a Wife' (1934), 'The Earlier Service' (1935) and 'The Curate and the Rake' (1935) are examples of some of her more widely anthologised tales. Outside of her fiction, in 1960 Irwin penned a well-regarded biography of Sir Walter Raleigh

MONSIEUR SEEKS A WIFE

MARGARET IRWIN

Note.—The following story is an extract from the private memoirs of Monsieur de St. Aignan, a French nobleman living in the first half of the eighteenth century.

I was twenty-four years of age when I returned in 1723 at the end of my three years' sojourn at the English Court, and had still to consider the question of my marriage. My father sent for me soon after my return and asked if I had yet given any thought to the matter. I replied that as a dutiful son I had felt it would be unnecessary and impertinent to do so. My father was sitting in his gown without his wig, for the day was hot, and as he sipped his chocolate he kept muttering, 'Too good—too good by half.'

I flicked my boots with my whip and did my best to conceal my impatience, for there was a hunt in the woods at Meudon and I feared I might miss it.

Presently he said, 'There was no one in England with whom you might have wished to form an alliance?'

'No, sir. The English actresses are charming.'

This time he seemed better pleased for he repeated, 'Good, good. That is an admirable safeguard to your filial duty in marriage.'

He then threw me over a letter from an old friend of his, the Comte de Riennes, a man of little fortune but of one of the oldest families in the kingdom. I skimmed two pages of compliments and salutations which seemed tedious to me after the shorter style of English correspondence, and got to the body of the letter. It was in answer to a proposal from my father that the two houses should be united by my marriage with one of the three daughters of the Comte.

He expressed warmly his gratitude and pleasure and told my father that as he had only enough fortune to bestow a *dot* on one of his daughters, the two others would enter a convent as soon as their sister was married; the choice of the bride he very magnanimously left to my father, and my father with equal magnanimity now left it to me. As I had seen and heard of none of them, I was perfectly indifferent.

'My motives are entirely disinterested,' I said to my father. 'I only wish to make a match that will be in accordance with your wishes and those of such an old friend of the family as Monsieur le Comte de Riennes. We had better therefore refer the choice back to him.'

As I said this, I turned the last page of the letter, and saw that Monsieur le Comte suggested that I should pay a visit to the Château de Riennes in the country of the Juras and see the three daughters for myself before deciding which I should marry. The generosity of this offer struck me forcibly and I at once accepted it. My father also remarked on the openness and liberality of his old friend, and observed that as in the usual course the eldest would have been appointed to the marriage, it would show justice and delicacy in me to choose her, unless of course she had a hump back or some other deformity; 'though in that case,' he remarked, 'she would surely have been placed in a convent long before.'

I went out to find that I was too late for the hunt at Meudon. It was the Regent* who informed me of this, for I met him strolling up and down one of the corridors in the palace and gaping out of the windows for all the world like an idle lackey. He was then very near the end of his life, though he was not old, and I remember being struck by his bloated aspect and thinking to myself, 'If that man should have a fit, I would not bet a button on his life.'

He did me the honour to ask me many questions about England, especially the rapid advance of scientific discovery in which he took a great interest.

'How times have changed!' he remarked. 'When I was young, I was regarded as a monster and a poisoner because I was an atheist and dabbled in chemistry. Also in black magic; it was the fashion then,' he added. "One must have some superstition, though I dare say you find it inconsistent to discard the superstition of religion, yet to retain that of sorcery.'

As he likes nothing so much as plain speaking, I owned to this, and added in explanation that in England the superstition of magic had for some time been confined to the ignorant and vulgar.

He then remarked on my approaching marriage (for my father had spoken of it to him) and, turning back just as he was leaving me, he said, The French Juras were a dangerous country once. Take care of yourself there.'

His voice always sounded as though he were joking, but his melancholy and bloodshot eyes looked serious. I knew that a savage country like the Juras was likely to be infested with robbers, but I should ride well attended and said so. The Regent only smiled, and it suddenly struck me as he walked away that the danger he was thinking of was not connected with robbers, and I could not guess what it was. I did not see him again before his sudden death, and three days later I set out on my journey.

The roads were bad and the inns worse, and I thought with regret of England, which seemed, especially at the worst inn, to be my adopted country. After an endless and dreary plain cultivated by wretched peasantry, I saw the rugged shapes of the Jura mountains against the sky and knew I was reaching my journey's end. The next day our horses were toiling steadily uphill, and the road was rougher, the countryside more deserted than ever. We entered a forest of dark pine trees which shed a gloomy twilight over our path, for it could now only by courtesy be termed a road. I began to be certain that we had missed our way, when I saw a creature approaching us who seemed to be human more from his upright position on two legs than from anything else in his appearance. I asked if we were on the road for Riennes, and though we had the greatest difficulty in understanding his dialect, it was at last clear that we were. He seemed, however, to be warning us not to take the wrong path farther on, and walked back a little way in order, I supposed, to direct us.

I dropped him some money for his trouble and he then repeated his warnings with what struck me as extraordinary urgency and even anxiety. He talked faster and more unintelligibly until the only word I could be certain of was the continual repetition of the name 'Riennes,' and he wagged his shaggy beard and rolled his eyes as he said it, with an expression that seemed positively that of fear or horror. I concluded that he was probably half-witted, and threw him another coin to get rid of him. At this he laid hold on my bridle and said two or three times, very slowly and as distinctly as he could. 'Do not go to Riennes.'

Convinced by now that the fellow was mad, I struck his hand off my bridle and rode on.

We came out of the forest to find ourselves surrounded by dark hills that rose sharply from the ground in jagged and hideous shapes. Their slopes were bare and uncultivated and many of their summits were crowned with frowning rocks. As I rode through this desolate and miserable country, a deep depression settled on me. I had for some time been feeling the regrets that most young men experience when the time comes for them to arrange their affairs and decide on marriage.

I was not yet sufficiently advanced in age or experience to consider youth and innocence the most attractive qualities in woman. But these would probably be the only charms in the raw country girl I was to marry, besides good health and perhaps rustic beauty.

I had heard much of the unutterable tedium of the lives of the smaller nobility on their country estates, a tedium only to be surpassed by the monotony of the religious life, which poverty enforces so large a proportion of our daughters and younger sons to enter.

Incongruously enough, I wondered at the same moment whether the eldest sister had red hands, and could have wept when it occurred to me that they might be no monopoly but general to all.

I thought with longing of my life and friends in London, of supper parties I had given on the stage, graced by the incomparable Mrs. Barry, the admirable Mrs. Bracegirdle, of the company at White's coffee-house where the conversation was often as good as in Mr. Congreve's comedies, of discussions on politics, philosophy, science, between men of wit and reason. But the melancholy that had now fastened on me was deeper than mere regret, and I could neither account for it nor shake it off.

We had to ask the way to Riennes more than once, and it struck me that the people who directed us showed more than the usual astonishment and awe natural to the peasant in an uncivilized country when suddenly confronted by a noble stranger and his retinue. In fact they seemed to show definite fear amounting sometimes even to terror, so that I was inclined to think that the old Comte must be a harsh and cruel lord to his people.

Towards evening we entered a gorge where our path went uphill between precipitous slopes and vast overhanging crags of dark rock. They were huger and more horrid than anything I could have imagined, and in the stormy twilight (for the clouds hung low and completely covered the taller hills) they presented an aspect that would have been terrifying to a weak and apprehensive imagination. We seemed no bigger than flies as our horses crawled up the steep ascent. A beetling crag overhung our path, and as I turned the sharp corner that it made, my mare suddenly reared and backed so violently that I was nearly thrown.

I urged her on with all my force and as I did so I glanced up and saw that what must have frightened her was the figure of a girl standing on the slope of the hill some way above us. She stood so still that at first glance she would have been indistinguishable from the rocks that surrounded her, had it not been for her long pale hair that the wind was blowing straight forward round her face. She wore a wreath of pale lilac and blue flowers, and I could just seize a glimpse of eyes that seemed the same colour as the flowers, set in a white face, before her hair blew past and hid it completely.

That glance was all I could give, for my mare was rearing and plunging in a manner utterly foreign to her usual behaviour. Suddenly, however, she stood quite still, trembling and bathed in sweat. I seized the opportunity to look up again, but the figure had gone. So still had she been while there, and so suddenly had she disappeared, that for an instant I doubted my senses and wondered if my eyes had played me some trick in that dim confusion of lights and shadows. But my impression of her had been too vivid for this doubt to last; I could even recollect the dark dress she wore, plainly cut like a peasant's. Yet I could not think of her as peasant, nor as a person of quality. She seemed some apparition from another world, and though I laughed at myself for my romantic fancy, I defy the most reasonable philosopher not to have shared it if he had seen her as I did. My mare certainly appeared to hold my opinion and with the greater conviction of terror, for she sidled most ridiculously past the place where the girl had stood, and was sweating and shivering as I rode her on. And what struck me as still more peculiar, all my men had some difficulty in getting their horses to pass that spot.

Half an hour later we were free of that hideous gorge, and could seen the towers of the Château de Riennes pointing upwards above the fir trees on the hill before us. Relief at reaching the end of my journey fought with an apprehension I could not understand. I remember an attempt at reassurance by telling myself, "If my wife plagues me, I can leave her on my estates in St. Aignan, and spend my time in London and Paris.' But even this reflection failed to encourage me.

We clattered into the courtyard to be met with acclamations from grooms and the lackeys who hurried forward to take our horses. The Comte himself came out to the steps of the château and stood awaiting me. He embraced me warmly and led me into the lighted hall with many expressions of welcome and friendship. He looked a much older man than I had expected in a comtemporary of my fathers, and his mild blue eyes certainly gave me no impression of the sternness I had anticipated from the timid behaviour of the peasantry.

Indeed there was a certain timidity in his own bearing, a weakness and vacillation in all his movements, as though he lived in continual and fearful expectation. But this did not in any way detract from the courtesy and cordiality of his reception of me and I might not have remarked it had I not been prepared for such a different bearing.

He led me to my room to remove the stains of travel and arrange my dress before being presented to the ladies of his family. Though early in the autumn the weather was cold, and a bright fire of pine logs blazed in my chimney. It was a relief to be sitting in a decent room once more, to have my riding-boots pulled off at last, and to put on a peruke that had been freshly curled and scented.

My valet was a useful fellow and. soon effected a satisfactory change in my appearance. I put on a suit of maroon-coloured velvet with embroidered satin waistcoat which I flattered myself set off my figure to advantage, and as I arranged my Mechlin ruffles before a very fine mirror, my gloomy apprehensions lifted, and it was with quite a pleasurable excitement that I looked forward to making the choice of my bride. I laughed at myself for my certainty that one or all would have ugly hands, and reflected that I should probably find a very good, pretty sort of girl and one that in this lonely place was not likely to be entirely unsusceptible.

Madame la Comtesse awaited me in a vast salon of a style that would have been old fashioned in the time of our grandfathers. The huge carved chair in which she sat, raised on a dais in semi-royal fashion at the end of the room, only served to make her appear the more insignificant. Her grey head was bowed, her long knotted fingers hung limply over the arms of her chair. But when she rose to greet me it was with the regal dignity that I remember my mother had told me quite old ladies had had in the days of her youth, a dignity that passed out of fashion with the late Queen Regent*, and is never seen now.

I was shocked, however, at the vacant yet troubled expression in her dim grey eyes. She certainly did not look as old as the Comte, nor could she, I knew from what my father had told me, be far past the period of middle life. Yet her mind seemed feeble and wandering as in extreme age.

She made me sit on a stool beside her chair and strove to entertain me with a courtesy that could still charm, though I could perceive very plainly the effort that it cost her. Every now and then she would stoop to caress a great white cat that rubbed against her chair and make some remark to it or to me concerning it.

I did my best to make friends with the favourite, but I do not like cats, and this beast regarded me with a distant and supercilious air, impervious to all my advances though it never took its pale green eyes off my face. This persistent stare irritated me till I longed to kick it out of the room, and foolishly this irritation somehow prevented me accommodating myself as well as I might have done to my hostess's tentative and desultory conversation.

It was a relief as well as an excitement when Mademoiselle de Riennes and Mademoiselle Marie de Riennes were announced. A tall girl entered the room with her arm around a light childish figure whose face was almost hidden against her sister's sleeve. The elder received my salutations with a certain amount of grace and finish, the younger with such confusion of shyness that in kindness I withdrew my eyes from her as soon as possible.

I was too anxious to see the elder to be able to see very clearly at first, but I perceived that she was neither ugly nor foolish and the hand I was permitted to kiss was of a good shape and colour. Later as we talked I saw that there were certain points in her face and figure that might be called beautiful. Her olive complexion lacked colour, but that could be easily remedied. She had large dark eyes of a very fine shape a well-formed bust and shoulders, a pretty mouth with good teeth, an excellent forehead and charming little ears. Yet the whole did not somehow make for beauty. It was incomplete or perhaps marred in some way.

It is difficult to perceive the habitual expression of a

young girl who is anxious to please, but I thought that the quick interest and smiles with which she attended to my conversation with her mother were not natural to her, and that from time to time a look of sullen and even fierce brooding would settle on her face, though momentarily, for the next instant she would rouse herself and seem to push it away.

Whenever I could do so without increasing her confusion, I stole a look at the younger daughter. She undoubtedly, was possessed of beauty, of a fair, almost infantile order; her lips were full and red and remained always just parted, her face was an exquisitely rounded oval, and her light-brown hair curled naturally on the nape of her neck in tendrils as soft and shining as those of a very young child. But she was extremely unformed, and I could not but feel that in spite of my vague disappointment in the elder, it was she who was in most respects the more suitable for my purpose.

After allowing sufficient time for her to compose herself, I addressed some simple remark to Mademoiselle Marie that should have been perfectly easy to answer. She looked at me with an uncertain, almost an uncomprehending expression in her blue eyes that reminded me of her mother's, and stammered a few words unintelligibly. Her extreme timidity was perhaps natural to her youth and upbringing, but I thought I detected a vacancy and weakness of mind in her manner of showing it.

'Decidedly,' I told myself, 'this one is best fitted for the convent, and after answering my remark myself as though I had but intended to continue it, I addressed myself again to the eldest. She replied very suitably and prettily and I thought her manners would not be amiss in any salon in London or Paris.

We continued happily therefore in a conversation which if not exactly amusing was at least satisfactory and promising, when an absurdly small incident occurred that proved oddly disconcerting to Mademoiselle.

The cat, which had so far continued to reserve its obnoxious gaze for me, suddenly walked across to her stool, looking up in her face and mewing. She shrank back with an involuntary shudder. It was not this that startled me, for I knew many people have an unconquerable aversion to cats and I have seen the great and manly Duc de Noailles turn faint at the Council Board because the little King[*] carried in a kitten. But what surprised me in Mademoiselle de Riennes was the same backward, fearful glance that I had seen in her father, as though she dreaded, not the cat itself, but some unseen horror behind her. The next moment, however, she was replying naturally and with no more than a becoming hesitation to some remark I had addressed to her.

I wondered why the third daughter had not appeared,

and the same wonder seemed to be disturbing my hostesses for they looked continually towards the door. Madame la Comtesse remarked two or three times, 'My daughter is late'; it was odd that she should so speak of her youngest daughter instead of reserving the expression for Mademoiselle de Riennes. She started violently when the footman announced, 'Mademoiselle Claude de Riennes,' and the eldest daughter leaned suddenly forward as though she would speak to me. She did not, but she fixed on me a look of such agonized entreaty that it arrested me as I rose, so that I did not turn on the instant, as I should have done, to greet Mademoiselle Claude.

When I did, I had to wait a full minute or two before I could recover sufficient composure to address her as I ought. Mademoiselle Claude was the girl I had seen on the rocky hillside. Her smooth and shining hair was dressed high in the prevailing fashion, her hooped dress of pearl-coloured satin was suitable to her rank, yet I was certain that she was the same as that wild figure I had seen, with hair blown straight before her face.

What further startled me was that I found that until that moment I had not really believed the apparition on the hillside to be a human creature. It was a disturbing discovery for a man of sense, living in an age of science and reason, to make in himself. I had certainly never before been guilty of imagining that I had seen a spirit.

I could only conclude that the peculiar gliding grace with which she advanced and curtsied to me did indeed connect her with the nymphs of mountain and grove in classic lore, and considered how I should turn a compliment to her on the subject without exposing to her family how I had met her in this strange fashion.

To my astonishment, however, she said in answer to her mother's introduction, 'I have already seen Monsieur de St. Aignan,' but no surprise was shown by mother or sisters. Mademoiselle Claude's voice was low and very soft, it had a quality in it that I have not met in any other voice and that I do not know how to describe; I should perhaps do so best if I said that it seemed to purr.

She sat beside her mother and did not speak again; her eyes were downcast and her long pale lashes, only less pale than her skin, languished on her cheek; her face was small and round, ending in a sharply pointed little chin. She wore in her bosom a bunch of the same light lilac and blue flowers that had been in her hair when I had first seen her, and the peculiarity of wearing such a simple posy when in full dress, caught my attention.

I asked their names, hoping to hear her speak again, but she only smiled, and it was the eldest daughter who told me that they were wild flowers, harebells and autumn crocuses, and that the latter with their long white stems and fainly purple heads were called Naked Ladies by the shepherd folk. Mademoiselle Claude raised her head as her sister spoke and handed me one to see. Her eyes looked full into mine for an instant and again I could not be certain if their pale colour were more like the blue or the lilac flowers, and again the compliment that rose to my lips evaded me before I could speak it.

The cat had deserted the chair of Madame la Comtesse and was rubbing backwards and forwards against Mademoiselle Claude, at last taking its eyes off my face and staring up at its young mistress. It was evident that she had no share of her sister's aversion to cats. Suddenly it leapt up on to her shoulder and rubbed its head against her long slim throat. Madame de Riennes stroked her daughter's head and that of the cat. 'They are both so white, so white, she murmured, and then, speaking I suppose to me, though she did not appear to be addressing anyone, she said, 'The moon shone on my daughter when she was born.'

I was embarrassed how to reply, for these disconnected remarks seemed to indicate premature senility more clearly than anything she had yet said. Fortunately at this moment the Comte entered and we went to supper.

I sat of course between my hostess and Mademoiselle de Riennes whom I wished to engage again in conversation. But her former ease seemed to have departed, she answered me with embarrassment and sometimes with positive stupidity. She now avoided meeting my eyes and looked repeatedly across the table to where her sisters sat opposite. I could not be sure which of the two she was looking at, for both sat silent with their eyes downcast.

The rest of the evening was spent in the salon, where Madame la Comtesse requested her daughters to show me some of the results of the labours that filled their days. Mademoiselle de Riennes led me to a tapestry frame that struck me as the most perfect exhibition of tedium that could be devised. Mademoiselle Marie showed me a Book of Hours that she was illuminating; my admiration was reserved for the fair fingers that pointed out their work. If the hands of Mademoiselle de Riennes were good, the hands of Mademoiselle Marie were delicious, not so fine in shape, but softly rounded, helpless and dimpled like a baby's. I began to wonder if I might not have judged nastily of her parts. Though the second in age, she appeared the youngest of the three; she was evidently slow in development, and who could tell but that after marriage had placed her in a suitable position, she might become the most brilliant as well as the most beautiful of all?

Politeness obliged me to turn at last to Mademoiselle Claude who was sitting as still as ever, with hands folded in her lap, and ask what she had to show me.

'Nothing, Monsieur,' said she, smiling, but without looking up.

'Mademoiselle is so idle?' I asked, hoping to tease her into a glance. But I did not win it, and at that moment Madame de Riennes suggested we should dance. It proved impossible as the daughters did not know the modern fashion of dancing and I knew no other. Madame de Riennes sat at the harpsichord and played an old-fashioned air to which her two elder daughters danced a *pas de deux*. I was surprised to see that again Mademoiselle Claude did not perform, and asked her if she did not like dancing.

'Oh, yes, Monsieur,' she replied, in that soft purring voice of hers, 'I like it very well.'

'Then do you not care to dance with two or three?'

'Monsieur is right, I prefer to dance with many.'

'Then, Mademoiselle, you can have but few opportunities for dancing here where I should imagine balls are a rarity. Do you not find it very dull?'

'No, Monsieur, I do not find it dull.'

All the time she seemed to be smiling, though as I was standing above her and her face remained lowered, I could not well see. The hands that lay so still in her lap were like the long white stems of the flowers she wore with the ridiculous name—they were so slim and bloodless. As I looked at them

I felt an unaccountable wish to draw away from them. I could in no way explain it; I have felt repulsion to hands before now, but to none that were beautiful. But I decided quickly that it was only an absurd fancy that likened them in my mind to hands of the dead, and so still and white they were that this was not surprising.

When the dance was finished, Madame de Riennes rose from the harpsichord and patted Mademoiselle Claude's cheek.

'My daughter can sing and play,' she said. 'She sits so still, too still, but she can sing very well.'

Mademoiselle Claude fetched her lute. As she sat with the instrument on her knee, her limp fingers plucking idly at the strings, I thought to myself, 'She is the last I would choose to be the mother of my heirs.' There seemed nothing alive about her, from her dead hair, so nearly white, to her pale and smiling lips. In the corner of the wainscot where she sat, her pearl-coloured skirts spread round her and reflected on the polished floor, she had the appearance of a moonlit cloud, possessing no doubt a certain strange beauty but more as a picture than a woman.

She began to sing; I did not think a great deal of her voice, having heard better, but it had a certain charm, being low, caressing and of a peculiar timbre. She sang an air from an opera now out of date, and then a song in which the tune was unlike any other I had ever heard. It was very simple and had a certain gaiety, it seemed to follow no known rules of method and harmony. There were two or three notes that recurred again and again like a call, and the melody between moved backwards and forwards as in the movement of a dance.

It seemed older than any other music, I cannot say why, unless it was that as I listened, my imagination conjured up visions of sacrificial dances performed in the most ancient times of Greece or Egypt. While in England, I had stayed at a country house whose owner had had the humour to take an interest in the old songs and ballads of his countryside and even to profess to admire them. He had played some of them to me one evening when he had tired of the cards, and I could not but admit that there was something in their rude simplicity that pleased the ear.

They were for the most part wild and plaintive, frequently unutterably dismal. But old as they had sounded, this tune that Mademoiselle Claude was singing seemed infinitely older. There was nothing plaintive in its wildness. It belonged to an age when men had not yet learned to regret, to distinguish between good and evil, to encumber themselves with the million hindrances and restrictions that separate men from beasts.

A strange restlessness and discontent seized on me. I

felt a ridiculous but none the less powerful loathing of my condition, of the condition of all men in this dull world, of the morals and customs that force our lives into a monotonous pattern from the cradle to the grave, of the very clothes I wore, stiff and cumbrous, crowned with a heavy peruke of false hair. I longed to fling them all off and shake myself free, and with them every convention that bound me to decency of conduct. In committing these words to paper, I am aware that I am describing the sensations of a lunatic and a savage rather than any that should be possible to a man of birth, sense and cultivation, living in a highly civilized and enlightened age. But if I am to be truthful in these memoirs I must admit that at the moment I failed completely to observe how shamefully, and, what perhaps is worse, how absurdly inappropriate my sentiments were to a gentleman and a courtier.

I raised my eves to find those of Mademoiselle Claude fixed upon my face. She was still singing, but I could not distinguish the words nor even recognize to which language they belonged. Her gaze did not startle me for I seemed to know that it had been resting on me for some time. I saw that her eyes, in this light at any rate, were neither blue nor lilac as I had thought, but pale green like those of the white cat that stood, arched and purring, on the arm of her chair; and, like the cat's, the pupils were perpendicular.

Heedless of manners, I looked hard to assure myself of the fact; and her eyes which had been so bashfully abased all the evening did not flicker nor turn away under my stare but continued to gaze into mine until I became conscious of nothing but their pale and luminous depths. They seemed to grow and to diminish, to come near and to recede very far away, and all the time the tune she sang moved up and down as in the measure of a dance, and the words she sang remained unintelligible yet gradually appeared to be familiar.

Suddenly the song ceased, and I started involuntarily and shook myself as though I had been rudely awakened from an oppressive dream. I looked around me, hardly able to believe that my surroundings had remained the same from the time when Mademoiselle Claude had begun to sing. Mademoiselle Marie, seated on a low stool next to her elder sister, was leaning so close against her that her face was completely hidden and her whole body was as stiff and motionless in its crouched position as if it had been paralyzed.

Mademoiselle de Riennes sat as still as she, but her eyes now raised themselves to mine slowly and with difficulty and I caught a glimpse of the same expression of agonized entreaty that had arrested me when I first rose to greet her youngest sister. It was only a glimpse, for the next instant they fell again as though not bearing to look longer into mine. In some way that I must fail to express, she appeared smaller and more insignificant. I wondered that I had ever thought of her as possessing good looks and distinction of manners.

Madame de Riennes had fallen into a doze and it may have been this that gave her, too, a slightly shrunken appearance. Certainly it struck me that she was much older and feebler than I had comprehended. I do not remember how I took my leave of them for the night, I only remember Madame la Comtesse murmuring weakly as she wished me good rest, 'She is so white, my daughter—too white, too white.'

The comfort of a good bed again after so long and uncomfortable a journey was by far my most important reflection on reaching my room, and as my valet prepared me for that blessed condition, the experiences and fancies of the past evening resolved themselves into the opinion that my imagination had been highly strung by the fatigues of the journey and the strangeness of new surroundings, and that in reality the family of the de Riennes were a very good, kindly, though old-fashioned sort of people, and that I had three pretty girls to choose from, though it was still a little difficult to know which to choose.

'Mademoiselle Marie is the prettiest,' I told myself on climbing into bed. 'But Mademoiselle de Riennes has the most sense,' I added, as Jacques drew the curtains round me, 'and Mademoiselle Claude'—I began as I laid my head on the pillows, but I found that I had not known what I thought of Mademoiselle Claude and was just dropping off to sleep without troubling to consider the question when I remembered that I had noticed something very strange about her eyes when she was singing.

For a moment I could not recall what it was, then suddenly it occurred to me, and with a sensation of horror that I had not felt at all at the time I had observed it, that the pupils of the eyes instead of being round were long and pointed.

I was exceedingly sleepy when I thought of this, but I woke myself by repeating several times as though it were of urgent importance that I should remember it—'The eyes are not human. Remember, the eyes are not human.'

I repeated it until I forgot what it was that had struck my observation, yet it seemed an imperative necessity that I should remember what it was that had filled my whole being with that sense of utmost horror. In my efforts to do so I fell sound asleep.

Nothing is more irritating than to be wakened out of a deep and dreamless slumber by some small, persistent noise. The noise I heard in my sleep kept awakening me again and again until at last, tired of perpetually dropping off and being aroused, I sat up in bed and listened. I heard something rustling outside my door, a soft running tread every now and then up and down the passage, and then, what I knew had awakened me so many times, something scratching at the door itself. I decided I must go and see what it was but felt the most absurd and shameful reluctance to do so.

I put out my hand through the curtains to reach for my bedgown on the chair beside me. Instead of the accustomed touch of velvet and fur that I expected, my hand seemed to be grasping a long cold finger. I recoiled in violent agitation, and as I snatched my hand away and covered it with my other as though to assure myself of a human touch, I thought I felt the finger drawn slowly across my forehead.

I shuddered from it, and yet my horror was mingled with an inexplicable pleasure. Trembling with excitement rather than with fear, I now drew aside the bed curtains, leapt out and opened the shutters.

The moon was nearly at the full, and by its brilliant light I could see, laid on my bedgown, the white and slender stalk of the wild autumn crocus that Mademoiselle Claude had presented to me. It surprised me, for I had no recollection of laying it there and indeed thought I had dropped it into the fire. In any case there was a satisfactory explanation of the cause of my ridiculous terrors, and the touch on my forehead must have been an imaginary result of them. It was odd, though, that as I took up the flower, the sensation of it seemed completely different from the thing that I had first grasped, and I marvelled that I could ever have mistaken it for a human finger.

All was so silent now that I got back into bed, first laying my sword on the chair beside me, and was just falling asleep when again I heard the rustle outside, and a soft stroking rather than scratching against my door. I stretched out my hand for the sword and found that it was shaking. This evidence of my womanish apprehension was so unaccountable and utterly confounding that I began to wonder if I were not already paying the price, though certainly an over-heavy one, of the pleasures naturally pertaining to a gallant man.

I resolved that now I was about to marry, I would make a different disposition of my life, abandon such pleasures, and settle on my country estates at St. Aignan. At this moment I heard that same furtive noise again on the door, and the idea that my plans for reforming were the result of the scratchings of a cat caused me to burst into a roar of laughter which wholesomely restored me to my natural self.

I snatched up my sword and ran to the door. I could see nothing but darkness, but I heard a faint 'miaow' somewhere down the passage and went quickly and cautiously towards it, calling 'Puss, Puss, Puss,' laughing to myself at the thought of the murder I was contemplating on the favourite of two of my hostesses, and already planning the apology I should have to make. The door into my moonlit room had swung to after me and I had to feel my way in the blackness. Suddenly

I felt claws round my leg and knew that the cat must have rushed at me from behind. I struck quickly down with my sword and thought I hit something soft and springing but could not be quite sure. There was no savage 'miaow' in response to show I had hurt the brute.

I went back to my room and on examining my sword in the moonlight, found that there was a small streak of blood on it. I thought with satisfaction that that would probably keep the beast away from my door, and settled myself for sleep. I was wrong, for all night I was disturbed by subdued sounds of scampering and scuffling in the passage, and more than once I thought that I felt the lightest pressure of a cold finger on my eyelids.

When Jacques brought me my chocolate in the morning, he found me more worn out and irritable than after a night of debauch. He exclaimed when he saw my sword on which the blood had dried, and I told him to clean it, saying that the cat had been disturbing my rest and that I had struck at it. My head throbbed and ached so uncomfortably that I decided I would refresh myself with a good ride before meeting any of my host's family, and ordered my mare to be saddled at once.

As I went down into the courtyard, I saw the white cat sleeping in a sunny corner of the steps. I turned the animal over with my boot, and it stretched out its paws and clawed playfully at the air. I could discover no sign of any wound anywhere upon it. I asked the groom what other cats they had, and he replied that this was the only one in the château. I got into the saddle, too much mystified to care to think, and rode as hard as I could.

The morning was fresh and pleasant, and the country looked excellent for boar-hunting. I was wondering what entertainment in that way my host meant to show me after my long abstinence (sport in England being of the tamest) when my attention was struck by a huge stone a little way off. I was riding across a fairly smooth slope of moorland with hills on my right that rose in abrupt and monstrous shapes as though thrown up by some violent cataclysm of the earth, while on my left stretched a vast plain as far as I could see. The whole was desolate because uncultivated, but in the morning sunshine the hideous aspect of the country did not oppress one as in the gloomy twilight in which I had first seen it. The stone I had noticed was conspicuous for its size and solitariness, for there were no rocks near.

I was riding up to it when suddenly my mare behaved in exactly the same manner as the evening before, shying violently and then rearing and plunging. I succeeded at last in quieting her sufficiently to keep still, but it was beyond my power to make her advance another step. I had always treated her with the consideration due to a lady of high breeding and mettlesome spirit, but on this occasion I must admit her whims drove me to a pretty considerable use of whip and spur. But all to no effect. She would not advance one step nearer the stone.

I dismounted and was about to see whether I could drag her thither by the bridle, when I noticed footprints at my feet, just in front of my mare's forefeet that were so obstinately planted on the ground. There was nothing odd in finding footprints on the moor, but what was odd was that they did not advance straight in any direction but curved sharply round. I followed them a little way and saw that the marks were exceeding confused, as though many pairs of feet had trodden close upon each other in the same spot. The grass, in fact, was all kicked up, and when I had followed this rough curve a little distance I saw that it was part of the outline of a vast circle in which the stone was, more or less accurately, the centre point.

I had no sooner made this perplexing discovery than I observed a respectable-looking man in black approaching me, whom I presently perceived to be a priest. He greeted me in an abrupt and not over-respectful fashion, asking if I were not afraid to go so near the fairy ring. Few people, he said, would care to adventure themselves so close to it even in broad sunlight. I observed, smiling, that the fairies in this part of the world must be remarkably substantial to have kicked up the ground so vigorously, and asked if he could not give me some more reasonable explanation of the footprints. He looked at me with a suspicious kind of sullen stupidity that made me conclude he was probably very little above the level of a peasant himself.

I left him to walk over to the stone, which I examined with some interest. The ground had been much disturbed close under it, and the stone itself, which was at the top like a table, was covered with dark stains. It occurred to me that here was a possible explanation of my mare's refusal to approach any nearer. Horses are notoriously sensitive to the smell of blood, and I was certain that the stains I was looking at were those of dried blood. I went back to the priest and asked him what the stone was used for.

'It is never used, Monsieur,' he cried, 'no one in the country would go near it.'

'Then,' said I, 'what are those dark stains on it?'

His little dark eyes looked at me anxiously and shiftily as though he disliked the subject.

'A holy man and a son of the Church, Monsieur, can know nothing of such things. Some say that this stone is haunted by devils and that they or the fairies, who resemble them dance in a ring round it.' He crossed himself and continued, 'I say that it is better not to speak of these things but to pray against temptation and the wiles of the Devil and to implore the help and protection of Holy Church.' He added that he was the *curé* of Riennes and chaplain to the convent near by, and invited me to look at his church which was not far off. I found myself walking with him, more out of inattention than politeness, my horse's bridle on my arm.

There was nothing to interest me in his church, a wretched chapel built at the rude Gothic period and even more chilly and uncomfortable than such buildings usually are.

I gave him something for his church, and mounting my mare, I rode back to the château.

I met one of the grooms at the gate, and throwing my bridle to him, walked through the gardens. As I had hoped, I saw the curve of a hooped petticoat on one of the seats, and hurrying towards it found Mademoiselle de Riennes and Mademoiselle Marie seated together, the younger reading her breviary aloud. Her hair caught reflections of gold in the sunlight in a way that enchanted me, and I lost no time in informing her of the fact in terms sufficiently metaphorical to be correct.

My compliments were received with a foolish stare, not even a blush to show they were comprehended. If a woman cannot take a compliment, she is lost. I turned to her sister to be met with better success, while the younger's attention returned to her breviary. Mademoiselle de Riennes tried to distract her from it, fearing, I think, that I might be offended.

'No, no,' replied the fair *dévote*, in an anxious and pleading manner, 'I promised Mother Abbess in Lianon I would always read first. But I will not disturb you by it—I can read elsewhere.'

She was about to rise but I sprang up from the grass where I had been setting at their feet and detained her.

'Do not, I beg of you, Mademoiselle,' said I, 'deprive me of an example as charming as it is edifying. I can never hope to see again such usually opposed qualities in such perfect conjunction.'

Then remembering that I was wasting my breath, I asked her as one would ask a child if she were very fond of the Mother Abbess she mentioned. She did not pay full attention to my question at first and I noticed a habit she continually had of brushing her hand across her eyes and then staring, as though she were not certain of what she saw. Then she answered, 'Oh, yes, very fond. One is safe with her.'

I glanced at Mademoiselle de Riennes to find how she took this odd remark, but was surprised that she seemed to have received it with an unreasonable amount of perturbation. She rallied herself quickly however, and said to me, My sister has always wished to enter the convent at Lianon, which is an order stricter than the convent here at Riennes. She has the vocation.'

I wondered whether Mademoiselle were entirely disinterested, in giving me this information, and I asked her what were her own feelings with regard to the conventual life. She replied in an even tone without a trace of that desire to please that had shown hitherto in all her remarks, 'That it is a useful necessity. That as it is no longer considered humane to expose newly-born daughters to the wolves on the hillside, their parents must be able to place them later in convents where they may die slowly, not from rigours and mortifications but from tedium, the tedium that makes all day and all night seem one perpetual and melancholy afternoon.'

Her eyes glittered with so strange an expression of hatred and even rage, that she, whom I had hitherto considered as the most reasonable of the family, now appeared almost wild. I wondered why her parents had not given her the right of priority which belonged to her, instead of leaving the choice to me.

My father's remarks on the subject came back to me, and I now considered that I had certainly better choose Mademoiselle de Riennes and satisfy the strictest claims of honour and delicacy. This decision was the easier to reach since Mademoiselle Marie had again shown so plainly she was a fool. I rose and took my leave of them that I might go and find the Comte to tell him my decision, for I feared that to wait too long before arriving at it might look like discourtesy.

I walked down an alley between clipped box hedges that rose above my head, and as I turned a corner I saw Mademoiselle Claude walking in my direction. She was correctly attired in a grey lute-string nightgown with ruffles of fine embroidery, her hands were folded in front of her and her head, slightly bent, was neatly dressed. When I had greeted her I asked if she had been walking long in the garden.

'No, Monsieur,' she replied, 'I have been to the convent. The chaplain informed me of your pious interest in his church.'

I disliked the thought mat the priest I had met was chaplain to the Convent of Riennes—still more, that he had been talking with Mademoiselle Claude. I asked her which of her sisters opinions she shared concerning the religious life—did she not agree with Mademoiselle de Riennes that it was inexpressibly tedious? She smiled very slightly.

'I should not find life in the convent tedious, Monsieur,' she said.

'Then you, like Mademoiselle Marie, have the vocation?'

'I have a vocation.'

As she spoke, she at last raised her eyes and looked up at me, nor did they flicker nor turn away as I looked down into them. It came upon me with a shock, that was not all displeasure, that the eyes of this young girl revealed a deeper knowledge of evil, which is what we generally mean by knowledge of life, than was sounded in all my experience as a travelled man of fashion. And as this struck me, I laughed, in a way that should have frightened her, but only brought her nearer to my side with a low, purring murmur, too soft for a laugh, her eyes still fixed on mine.

An extraordinary sensation swam over me. I was trying to remember something that I had seen in or thought about her eyes the evening before. The effort to remember was so strong that it was like a physical struggle, and though I felt I might succeed if I drew my eyes away from hers for a moment, I could not do this.

Then I noticed that she was humming the tune of the song that she had sung the night before, and as she did so her body rocked a little, backwards and forwards, as though swaying to the measure of a dance, while her eyes never left mine. I advanced a step towards her, she receded, we seemed to be dancing together, though with what steps and movement I could not say. Presently she was speaking to me, chanting the words of the tune—'Monsieur enjoys dancing? Monsieur will dance with me?'

I seized her by the shoulders. She winced and cried out, her lips contorted with pain that my movement, rough as it was, could not have caused by itself. As she tried to pull herself away, her dress slipped over her shoulder and revealed a freshly made scar on the white skin, caused by a knife or some other weapon. I cried out on seeing it and let go of her, but she pulled her dress over it again in an instant, looking back over her shoulder at me and smiling.

'So Monsieur will dance with me,' she said, and moved away from me down the alley so quickly that she seemed to have gone before I had perceived her go.

I was now utterly unwilling to continue my way to the château, to tell the Comte I desired to marry his eldest daughter. I roamed up and down the box alleys for a considerable length of time, ill at ease and dissatisfied. The rest of the day passed in an intolerable mingling of tedium and excitement. I seemed to be waiting for it to pass in eager expectancy of I knew not what. I found myself watching the sun as though I were longing for it to set; again and again I glanced at the dock and told myself, 'The moon will be at the full tonight,' though I did not know what possible interest that could have for me.

I supposed it was some echo of Madame la Comtesse's maundering fancies when she had rambled to me about her youngest daughter, and I tried to pull myself up sharply and point out mat I was myself becoming like an old woman, my mind incapable of decision or reasoning, of anything but a feeble repetition of words and phrases that, came from I knew not where.

Yet I could not shake off this mood nor discover what I meant to do regarding my marriage; nor indeed what I was thinking of. I found conversation, even with Mademoiselle de Riennes, unbearably wearisome; it was no pleasure to observe Mademoiselle Marie's beauty which now appeared as insipid and lifeless as a puppet's. I saw Mademoiselle Claude again only in the presence of her parents, but she never spoke nor did she look at me.

In the evening I chanced to be alone with the Comte. I felt that he was expecting me to speak of my marriage, and suddenly I knew that it was only his youngest daughter I had any desire to marry—a desire so burning and importunate that I marvelled I had not realized my wishes sooner. I spoke of them, saying that though I was anxious to perform the part of a man of scrupulous honour, I could not but take advantage of his liberality and make my choice according to the dictates of my heart.

He showed no surprise, and gave his consent in terms appropriate and correct, with nothing that I could interpret as expressive of displeasure. Yet he spoke mechanically and with a strained, uneasy attention, almost, or so it sometimes appeared, as if he were listening and repeating someone else's words, instead of directly answering me. It struck me when he had finished speaking, that he was a smaller and a duller man than I had formerly observed him to be.

I found a pretext for going early to my room, where I paced up and down in a fever of restlessness. In spite of the exaltation of my new desires and the immediate prospect of their fruition, I felt that I had never been so much bored in the course of my whole existence as at that moment; that never before had I discovered how ineffably tedious and wearisome that whole existence had been.

I remembered the various pleasures I had experienced and marvelled that I had ever found zest in them; my deepest passions, my most exciting adventures, now appeared as flat, trivial and insipid as the emotions and escapades of a schoolboy. I wondered with a kind of despair if there were nothing left in life that could amuse me. The fact that my marriage was to be one of inclination should no doubt have answered this question, but I seemed already satiated with that as with all else.

I would have bartered all that was most dear to me, my possessions, my name, my life, my honour, my soul itself, for any new experience that could satisfy this new curiosity and raise me from my intolerable tedium. Desires arose in me so monstrous and unnatural that my thoughts could scarcely find shape or name for them, yet I regarded them calmly, without horror, without even surprise.

At last I went to bed, because however much I longed to

be occupied there was no other occupation for me. In spite of the disordered turmoil in my brain, I fell asleep quickly. No noises disturbed me this time, I did not dream, but I woke as suddenly as I had fallen asleep. I drew back my bed-curtains and saw that the room was full of moonlight, for the window shutters which Jacques had closed before he left me for the night were now wide open, and I could hear a great noise of wind in the pine trees outside. In the middle of the floor stood the white cat, perfectly still, its back arched and tail erect, its pale green eyes glaring at me. It now leaped on to the foot of the bed and began ramping its paws up and down on the quilt in a state of violent excitement, uttering short wild mewing cries.

I kicked it off, but it sprang on to another part of the bed and clawed at the bed-clothes as though trying to pull them off. A cloud must have passed over the moon for the room was momentarily darkened, and a blast of wind came roaring through the pines and rushed in through my open shutters, blowing the bed-curtains all over me. In that instant I could have sworn that I felt the light cold touch of a hand on my heart.

I scrambled out of bed and hurried on my clothes as though my life depended on getting dressed instantly. Clapping on my sword-belt I strode to the door and found the cat there awaiting me. It was purring loudly, and looking back to me if I was following, it trotted into the passage. I could just see a vague shape of something white as it passed before me through the darkness and I followed downstairs and along passages until I came plump against a closed door. I fumbled for bolts and locks and unfastened them, hearing always the purring of the cat close by me. It never occurred to me to wonder why I was following this beast I detested, out of doors in the middle of the night.

As soon as the door was open I hurried out as fast as I could, through the gardens and out on to the countryside. I was not following the cat now, nor did I see it anywhere. I did not know where I was going, but presently I perceived that I was on the same broad slope of moorland where I had ridden that morning. There were sharp risings and fallings in the ground that I had avoided in my ride, and that prevented my seeing far in front; also, though the moon when unclouded shone clear in the sky, a low-lying miasmic fog obscured the ground.

As I rose to the summit of one of these mounds, I stopped and listened. I thought that I had heard music, but as the wind rushed onwards through the pine woods behind me, I could no longer distinguish it. At this moment the whole light of the full moon shone out from behind a hurrying cloud, and I saw vaguely before me in the mist a vast circle of apparently human figures, revolving in furious movement round some huge and dark object of fantastic shape. Clouds of smoke, reddened now and then by fire, rose round this object and were swept onwards in the wind.

I ran towards the circle; as I did so, the music came nearer, now loud, now faint, on the uncertain blast, and I recognized the tune as the same that Mademoiselle Claude had sung to me. I approached cautiously as I drew near. Sometimes the ring of dancers swung so near me that I was within a few feet of them, sometimes it receded far away. All the figures were holding hands and faced outwards, their backs toward the centre of the circle that they formed.

I saw the figures of men, women and even children flying past me; not one had a human face. The faces of goats, toads, cats, of grinning devils and monkeys, showed opposite me for one instant, clear in the moonlight or obscured by the drifting smoke. Those that seemed most horrible of all were white faces that had no features.

Suddenly the ring broke for one instant as it swung within a yard of where I crouched, and at that moment a blinding cloud of smoke blew into my face. A hand was flung out and touched mine, a light cold touch that I knew. I seized it and sprang to my feet, inmediately my other hand was clasped and I was swung madly onwards into the movement of the dance.

I could now no longer see the dancers, not even those on

either side of me whose hands I grasped. I saw nothing but the night, the smoke, the flying landscape, now vague and vast as of an illimitable sea of fog, now black and hideous shapes of mountains that rose sharply in the moonlight. I felt an exhilaration such as I had never known, a brusque and furious enjoyment, as though my senses and powers were quickened beyond their natural limit. Yet again and again I found I was trying to remember something, with the urgency and even the agony that besets one in a nightmare; but my mind appeared to have forsaken its office.

Then without any warning the hands in my clasp were torn from me, and the ring broke in all directions. I staggered back unable to keep my balance in the shock of the suddenly loosened contact; the next instant I realized that she who had first taken my hand had gone, and I was hunting madly for her through that monstrous assembly.

Though the ring had broken, the music continued, and I jostled many who were still dancing, back to back, with their hands joined. In the misty confusion it was impossible to distinguish anything clearly; I thought I saw gigantic toads dressed in green velvet who were carrying dishes, but I did not stay to remark them. Huge clouds of dun-coloured smoke arose before me, lit up momentarily by flames, and in their midst I saw for an instant a shape that seemed greater and more hideous than the human. A mighty voice arose from it, speaking, it seemed, some word of command, and straightaway all the company fell on their knees.

Then I saw her whom I had been seeking. She stood erect on what appeared to be a black throne, the fiery smoke behind her. The moon, darkened of late, shone out on her white limbs that were scarcely concealed by the fluttering rags she wore. Her loosened hair blew straight before her face, and appeared snow-white in the moonlight. Something gleamed in her uplifted hand, she bent, and at this moment an awful cry arose, a sobbing shriek so deformed by its extreme anguish and terror that though it was certainly human I could not distinguish if it were from man, woman or child. The figure rose erect, her arms flung wide as in triumph, her face revealed. It was the face of Mademoiselle Claude.

I rushed towards the throne; it was the huge stone I had observed on my ride. She turned towards me, her face bent down to greet me, her lips parted in laughter, her eyes gleaming as I had never seen them, her whole body transfused with some mysterious force that seemed to fill her with life, pleasure and attraction more than human. My senses reeled as in delirium, I seized her in my arms and dragged her from the stone. In doing so, my hand closed on the knife in hers, and something warm and wet drenched my fingers. The meaning of that hideous death-cry I had just heard suddenly penetrated my numbed and stupefied brain—and I stood stiff with horror, cold sweat breaking out on my hands and forehead.

She twisted herself in my arms till her face looked up into mine; her eyes shone like pale flames and appeared to draw near and then recede very far away, and with them my horror likewise receded until I felt I was forgetting the very cause of it. Yet it seemed to me, as though someone not myself were telling me, that if I did so, the consequences would be worse than death. I struggled desperately to recall what I had felt, and with it something else that all that past day and this night I had been trying to remember. I longed to pray but was ashamed to enlist the aid of a Power that until that moment I had doubted and mocked.

Her arms slid upwards round my neck; my flesh shuddered beneath their embrace as from contact with some loathsome thing, yet she seemed but the more desirable. My consciousness began to fail me as I bent over her. Again the eyes came close, enormous, and I stared at the pupils, black and perpendicular in their green depths. A voice that I did not at first recognize for my own shrieked aloud—'They are not human. Remember, the eyes are not human.'

As I cried out, I found that I could remove my eyes from hers, I looked down at what I held, and on her naked shoulder saw the scar I had observed that morning. I knew now that it had been made by my own sword the night before when I had struck in the darkness at her familiar, and the discovery turned me sick and faint. I frantically repulsed the accursed white body that clung to mine, and made to draw my sword. The witch screamed not in fear but in laughter, and flung herself upon me with her knife before I could get my sword free from its scabbard. I fended off the blow on my heart, and with my left arm dripping blood I seized her wrist while my right, now holding my sword, was raised to strike.

In that instant I was seized from behind by what seemed to be a hundred slippery hands clawing at my neck, arms and ankles. The whole mob, laughing, sobbing, screaming, chuckling, was round me and upon me. It appeared certain that I should be overcome, but I struck out madly with my sword and succeeded in effecting some clearance round me.

A kind of berserker fury consumed me; I rushed upon that obscene herd, striking right and left to hew a passage through them. They fled shrieking in front of me but closed on me from behind; I was bitten, clawed, scratched, hacked at, cut at, with no proper weapons it seemed, but the blows would have been sufficient to overcome me had not all my forces been so desperately engaged.

After a period that seemed to endure for hours, I found that I was hacking blindly at the empty air; I wiped the blood from my eyes and looking round me saw that I was alone, surrounded only by the mounds and hillocks through which I had approached to that frightful merrymaking. My legs would no longer support me, my senses fled from me, and I fell upon the ground.

I woke to consciousness to see the light of dawn behind the mountains. All was silent; at some distance, a thin column of smoke, as from a dying fire, ascended straight upwards in the still air. I struggled to my feet and with all the strength that was left in my bruised body I dragged myself towards the château.

One of my grooms was in the courtyard as I entered, and cried out on seeing my condition. I cut him short and ordered him to assemble the rest of my band and have my horses saddled with the utmost expedition. I commanded Jacques to leave all my baggage and we were ready for departure, before any of the Comte's household, excepting the servants, were aroused.

In raw and foggy daylight we rode out of the courtyard and down the road that led from Riennes.

I will finish this event in my memories here, though I must traverse six years to do so. The other day, while on a protracted visit to London, I was sitting in White's coffee-house when Jacques brought me the papers that I have sent me regularly from France. In one of them was a notice which so much engaged my attention that I lost all account of the conversation around me. My Lord Selborne asked me what news I found so engrossing. I read aloud: 'In the French Juras a nun, youngest daughter of the ancient and noble family of R——, has been tried and found guilty of sorcery. She was burnt at the stake. The nun's two sisters are also in the religious life, and the eldest, who is in the same convent, fell under suspicion for some time but has been cleared. In fact so many arrests were made both within the convent and through the whole countryside that it was found impossible to prosecute them all, lest the whole district of R——, the scene of these horrors, should require to be burnt.'

Here my lord interrupted me with expressions of horror that France, even in her remotest provinces, should still be so barbarously superstitious as to burn a woman of quality for a witch.

'In England,' he remarked, 'we got over such whimsies in the time of the Stuarts, and since then the women, God bless 'em, have been allowed to enchant with impunity.'

That very able man, Monsieur Voltaire the playwright, who was then on his visit to England, burst forth in great indignation against the priest-ridden laws of our country that could make such executions possible. What could it matter, he declared, if an ignorant peasantry, rebelling against the tedium of its miserable existence, cared at certain seasons to make a bonfire, dress up one of their number as the Devil, put masks on the rest, and indulge in the mummery of the Witches' Sabbath?

In his grandfather's day, sorcery had been a fashion extending even to the *noblesse* and gentry; the trial of La Voisin, the famous sorceress and prisoner, had implicated hundreds, even, it was whispered, the King's reigning sweetheart, Madame de Montespan herself. Whole villages, indeed whole districts in the Basques and Juras, had been devastated by the laws against witchcraft, and it had proved impossible to deal with all the witches that had been arrested.

'But witchcraft amounted to more than mummery,' declared one Mr. Calthrop. 'On my own estate in my father's time a stone was thrown at an old woman's dog and the mark was found on *her* body.'

Monsieur Voltaire waved this aside. He had heard many such instances and did not deny that there was foundation for them. Such people as believed themselves to be witches were certainly abnormal, and they, and the animals they used as their ministers, might well have abnormal powers. But he was certain that the world did not yet fully realize the powers of thought and belief. He considered it possible that future ages would attribute such instances of unnatural sympathy between a witch and her familiars to an unnatural state of mind and body. He addressed his remarks chiefly to me, but I did not answer them.

In spite of the fact that as I am now approaching my thirty-first year, middle age is hard upon me, I have still to find a wife to carry on my family.

THE WITCH CHARMER

'I will relate to you some examples, which I have gained in part from the teachers of our faculty, in part from the experience

of a certain upright secular judge, worthy of all faith, who from the torture and confessions of witches and from his experiences in public and private has learned many things of this sort—a man with whom I have often discussed this subject broadly and deeply—to wit, Peter, a citizen of Berne, in the diocese of Lausanne, who has burned many witches of both sexes, and has driven others out of the territory of the Bernese. I have moreover conferred with one Benedict, a monk of the Benedictine order, who, although now a very devout cleric in a reformed monastery at Vienna, was a decade ago, while still in the world, a necromancer, juggler, buffoon, and strolling player, well known as the delight of village children everywhere.

From the 15th century *Formicarius* of Johannes Nider, the Dominican theologian who provided the clue that magic might form the basis of one of the most famous of all German legends. . . .

* Duke of Orleans, Regent of France during the minority of Louis XV.

* Anne of Austria, mother of Louis XIV and Regent of France during his minority.

* Louis XV.